Can You Solve the Mystery?™

Hawkeye Collins & Amy Adams in

The Secret of the

Long-Lost

Cousin

& 9 Other Mysteries

Created by Bruce Lansky

🐢 Meadowbrook Press
Distributed by Simon & Schuster
New York

Library of Congress Cataloging-In-Publication Data

This title was previously cataloged with the following information: Masters, M.
Hawkeye Collins & Amy Adams in the secret of the long-lost cousin and other mysteries.
At head of title: Can you solve the mystery?™
Summary: The reader is asked to help two twelve-year-old sleuths, "Hawkeye" Collins and Amy
Adams, solve ten mysteries using Hawkeye's sketches of important clues.
[1. Mystery and detective stories. 2. Literary recreations.] I. Title. II. Title:
Secret of the long-lost cousin and other mysteries.
PZ7.M42392Hk   1983   [Fic] 83-5392

ISBN: 978-1-4424-6899-3

Editor: Kathe Grooms
Assistant Editor: Louise Delagran, Alicia Ester
Cover Design: Tamara JM Peterson
Design: Stephen Cardot, Terry Dugan
Production: John Ware, Donna Ahrens, Pamela Barnard, Daryl Peterson
Illustrations: Stephen Cardot
All stories written by Alexander von Wacker

17 16 15 14 13 12   10 9 8 7 6 5 4 3 2

Printed in USA

Contents

Amy Adams   Hawkeye Collins

Young Sleuths Detect Fun in Mysteries

By Alice Cory
Staff Writer

Lakewood Hills has two new super sleuths watching over its citizens. They are Christoper "Hawkeye" Collins and Amy Amanda Adams, both 12 years old and sixth-grade students at Lakewood Hills Elementary.

Christopher Collins, the popular, blond, blue-eyed sleuth

of 128 Crestview Drive, is better known by his nickname. "Hawkeye." His father, Peter Collins, who is an attorney downtown, explains, "We started calling him Hawkeye many years ago because he notices everything, even tiny details. That's what makes him so good at solving mysteries." His mother, Linda Collins, a real estate agent, agrees: "Yes, but he

Sleuths continues on page 4A

Sleuths continued from 1A

also started to draw at a very early age. His sketches capture everything he sees. He draws clues or the scene of the crime — or anything else that will help solve a mystery."

Amy Adams, a spitfire with red hair and sparkling green eyes, lives right across the street, at 131 Crestview Drive. Known to many as the star of the track team, she is also a star math student. "She's quick of mind, quick of foot and quick of temper," says her teacher, Ted Bronson, chuckling. "And she's never intimidated." Not only do she and Hawkeye share the same birthday, but also the same love of mysteries.

"If something's wrong," says Amy, leaning on her bike, "you just can't look the other way."

"Right," says Hawkeye, pulling his ever-present sketch pad and pencil from his back pocket. "And if we can't solve a case right away, I'll do a drawing of the scene of the crime. When we study my sketch, we can usually figure out what happened."

When the two detectives are not playing video games or soccer (Hawkeye is the captain of the sixth-grade team), they can often be seen biking around town, making sure justice is done. Occa-sionally aided by Hawkeye's frisky golden retriever, Nosey, and Amy's six-year-old sister, Lucy, they've solved every case they've handled to date.

How did the two get started in the detective business?

It all started last year at Lakewood Hills Elementary's Career Days. There the two met Sergeant Treadwell, one of Lakewood Hills' best-known policemen. Of Hawkeye and Amy, Sergeant Treadwell proudly brags, "They're terrific. Right after we met, one of the teachers had a whole pile of tests stolen. I sure couldn't figure out who had done it, but Hawkeye did one of his sketches and he and Amy had the case solved in five minutes! You can't fool those two."

Sergeant Treadwell adds: "I don't know what Lakewood Hills ever did without Hawkeye and Amy. They've found a dognapped dog, located stolen video games, and cracked many other tough cases. Why, whenever I have a problem I can't solve, I know just where to go — straight to those two super sleuths!"

> **" They've found a dognapped dog, located stolen video games, and cracked many other tough cases. "**

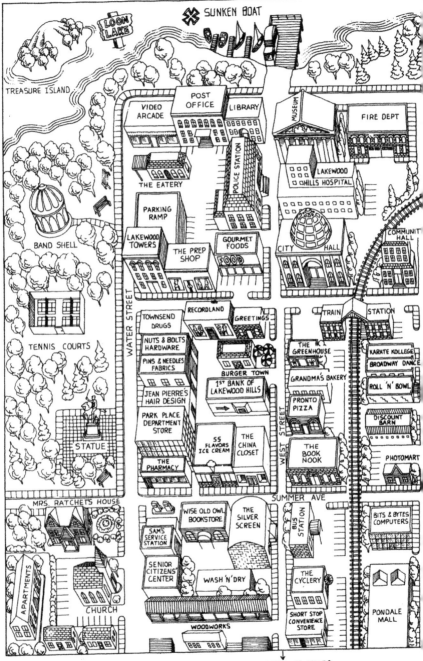

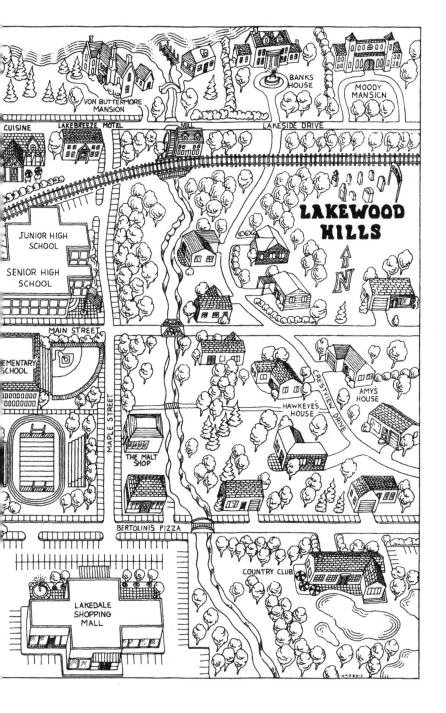

Dear Readers,

    You can solve these mysteries along with us! Start by reading very carefully —— Watch out for things like what people <u>say</u> happened, the ways they behave, and details like the time and the weather.

    Then look closely at the sketch or other picture clue with the story. If you remember the facts, the picture clue should help you break the case.

    <u>If</u> you want to check your answer—— or if a hard case stumps you —— turn to the solutions at the back of the book. They're written in mirror type. Hold them up to a mirror and they'll look right. If you don't have a mirror, turn the page and hold it up to the light. (You can teach yourself to read backwards, too. We can do it pretty well now and it comes in handy some-times in our cases.)

    Have fun —— we sure did!

Hawkeye   Amy

The Secret of the
Long-Lost
Cousin

Seated at the dining room table, Hawkeye glanced over at his father.

"Dad," he said as he speared the large pile of spaghetti on his plate, "what happened to those three grey hairs above your right ear?"

His father coughed. "Ahem, Hawkeye, you have a lot of homework tonight, don't you?"

Almost effortlessly, Hawkeye began to twirl the long noodles onto his fork. "But, Dad, I remember seeing them yesterday. Three little grey hairs."

Mrs. Collins looked in amazement at her husband. "Why, you didn't..." She started to laugh. "You pulled them out, didn't you?"

Mr. Collins' face turned red. "Oh, all right. I might as well confess. Yes, I pulled them out." He smiled and looked at his son. "Hawkeye, why do you have to be so darn observant all the time?"

"Beats me." Hawkeye shrugged. "I just can't help it."

With a flick of his wrist, he had a neat serving of spaghetti noodles on his fork. It was the same coordinated movement that enabled Hawkeye to be the undisputed school video game champ. But before he put them in his mouth, he was struck by a great idea.

"Wow," he said, leaning over the table toward his parents. "I just thought of something: a meatball and spaghetti video game! Now, that'd be weird."

"Yes, I suppose it would," said Mr. Collins. "But let's talk about your homework. You're going to have to get a lot done tonight if you want to watch the World Cup game on TV tomorrow night."

"And don't forget you have a piano lesson tomorrow," his mother added. "You really should practice—you could play wonderfully if you only put some time into it."

Hawkeye stopped twirling the noodles. "But—"

Just then the doorbell rang. Nosey, Hawkeye's golden retriever, jumped up so fast from under the table that she bonked her head. She barked loudly and bounded toward the front door.

Happy to change the subject, Hawkeye dropped his fork. "I'll go see who it is." He raced after Nosey.

"It's okay, Nosey," he said to the excited dog.

Hawkeye wiped the last traces of spaghetti sauce from his mouth with the back of his hand and swung open the front door. A man about his parents' age stood on the doorstep with a briefcase in his left hand. Nosey greeted the man by beating her tail back and forth like a windshield wiper out of control.

"Hi," said Hawkeye. "Is there something I can do for you?" He wondered if the man were a politician out campaigning.

A big, hopeful smile appeared on the man's face. "This is the Collins house, isn't it?"

"Yes." Hawkeye figured that the man was a salesman instead.

The stranger roughly shook Hawkeye's hand. "Then you must be Christopher!" He took a step forward and gave Hawkeye a bear hug. Hawkeye stiffened in response.

"Hawkeye," called his father from the dining room. "Who is it?"

Hawkeye squirmed out of the man's arms. "I don't know, Dad. I think you'd better come see." He grabbed Nosey, who was sniffing the man's briefcase. "Cut it out, Nosey. Come back in here."

The dog trotted back into the house. A moment later, Hawkeye's parents came to the door.

"Can I help you?" asked Mr. Collins.

"Ohhh, I'm so happy!" said the stranger loudly. He stepped forward, wanting to shake hands with Mr. and Mrs. Collins.

"My name is Dan," he said, his voice booming. "At last I've met you." He grasped Mrs. Collins' hand in both of his and shook it. "Oh, cousin!"

Mrs. Collins was shocked and almost speechless. "Cou... cousin?"

"Yes. Virginia, your mother, and Elizabeth, my mother, were sisters. My parents eloped and homesteaded in Alaska. We've always wanted to come back and see you but we couldn't afford it. But finally, here I am!"

It took Mrs. Collins a moment to recover. "Well... well, won't you come in?" she said, opening the door fully.

They returned to the dinner table and served Dan a large plate of spaghetti.

"Wow, Mom, this is incredible, isn't it?" said Hawkeye. "A long-lost cousin shows up from out of the blue."

Mrs. Collins was still surprised by the news. "Yes," she said slowly, "Mother used to talk about her only sister, Elizabeth, who had moved to Alaska. She used to call her the pioneer because she and her husband moved into the wilderness. If I'm correct, they didn't even have a phone or electricity. Mother would get letters at Christmas."

"That's right. We heard about you, too, and Christopher here," said Dan.

"You can call me Hawkeye. Everybody does," said Hawkeye politely.

"Oh, excuse me, Dan. Let me get you a salad. I'll be right back." Mrs. Collins stood and went into the kitchen.

"Hey," said Hawkeye, pulling at the neck of his red t-shirt. "Did you hear very much about us when you were growing up?"

"Sure," said Dan as he ate hungrily. "We heard a lot about you. My mother always used to tell me how her older sister, Virginia, used to take care of her."

With some difficulty, Dan clumsily twirled some spaghetti onto his fork and tried to get it into his mouth before it all fell off.

"Hawkeye, one time your grandmother was baby-sitting and pushing my mother in the stroller. She got tired of pushing, so she hitched the stroller to the dog. But then the dog saw a cat and took off, pulling the stroller behind. They finally caught the dog after three blocks. Luckily, Elizabeth didn't get hurt."

Hawkeye laughed. "Hey, Amy—she's my friend who lives across the street—did the same thing to her kid sister, Lucy!"

Dan chuckled. "It probably happens all the time."

"So, when did you get here?" asked Hawkeye.

"My plane got in from Anchorage just this evening. I tried to call but you weren't home, so I rented a car and came out anyway."

"What brings you to town?" asked Mr. Collins.

"I'm here on business. I'm looking into some hot investments."

Mrs. Collins came in carrying a salad for Dan. "Do you have a place to stay?"

"Oh, yes, I have a hotel room downtown. I hope, though, that I'll be able to see you again."

"I hope so, too," said Mrs. Collins. "Say, why don't you come for dinner tomorrow night, too?"

"Great. By then, I might be able to tell you about these investments. You may be interested. But meanwhile, I've got something for you, Hawkeye."

Dan reached down and opened his briefcase. A chocolate bar fell out, and Nosey, sniffing the air and wagging her tail, hurried over. Dan picked up the candy and then took out a book.

"Here, Hawkeye," he said, "this is for you. It's a book of magic tricks. I'll show you tomorrow how you do some of the tricks."

"Great!" said Hawkeye, opening the book.

"Well, it has been an exciting evening," said Mr. Collins, "but it's getting late and I believe someone has homework to do. Hawkeye, I'll load the dishwasher for you tonight, but you've got to get right to work if you want to visit with Dan tomorrow, learn magic tricks, and watch the soccer game."

"Well, I guess you have a point, Dad. Here goes." Hawkeye stood up. He realized that at least he wouldn't have to practice the piano. To Dan he said, "See you tomorrow."

Hawkeye headed to his room. "Imagine," he thought to himself, his mind not on his homework, "a long-lost cousin just showing up out of nowhere. Sure seems strange." He sat down, reluctantly put aside the magic book, and opened his math book to study for a test.

Well over an hour later, his father peeked in. "How's the studying going?"

Hawkeye yawned. "Okay, I guess."

Mr. Collins came over and hugged him. "It's getting late. Time to hit the hay. And don't forget to brush your teeth. Night, son."

"Night, Dad. Are you gonna watch the game with me tomorrow night?"

"Well, I'll see what Dan wants to do."

Hawkeye's mother came in and kissed him. "Night, dear. Night, Nosey."

"Night, Mom."

"Dad's going to bed and so am I," said his mother. "Lights out for you, too. Right away."

"Sure, Mom," said Hawkeye as he took off his socks. "I just have to brush my teeth."

Hawkeye got ready and climbed into bed. He patted Nosey, who was already curled up next to the bed, and then turned out the light. But he kept thinking about the long-lost cousin. And the more he thought, the stranger it seemed.

Hawkeye tossed and turned sleeplessly for nearly an hour. Suddenly, he remembered an old family photograph his grandmother had given him. He climbed out of bed and picked up his flashlight. He was pretty sure the photograph was in the living room and he wanted to find it.

A moment later, flashlight in hand and followed by Nosey, Hawkeye tiptoed down the dark hall. He froze near his parents' bedroom door when he heard his father cough. When all was quiet, Hawkeye headed on to the living room. He carefully sneaked through the large, dark room over to the tall bookcase.

After a few moments of searching, Hawkeye found a large photo album. He turned the large pages until he came to an old, brownish photograph of his grandmother's family.

By the beam of his flashlight, Hawkeye studied the photograph. Then he read the note his mother had written on the edge of the picture.

GRANDMA AS A BABY IN HER MOTHER'S ARMS

By the beam of his flashlight, Hawkeye studied the photograph.

"Wow, look at this!" said Hawkeye in surprise. "I *knew* something was wrong! This picture proves that Cousin Dan is a fake."

WHAT DID HAWKEYE SEE IN THE PHOTOGRAPH THAT PROVED "COUSIN DAN" WASN'T A COUSIN?

The Case of the
Disappearing
Diamonds

"Hawkeye!" There was an unmistakable note of urgency in Sergeant Treadwell's voice as it came over the telephone line.

"There's just been a big jewelry theft up at the von Buttermore mansion and I need a drawing of the scene of the crime. Do you suppose you and Amy could come up right away?"

"Sure, Sarge." Ever since Hawkeye and his friend, Amy Adams, had met Sergeant Treadwell at Lakewood Hills Elementary's Career Day, they had helped him solve many cases. Hawkeye's sharp eyes and accurate sketches and Amy's quick thinking made them a great pair of detectives.

"Great. I knew I could count on you and Amy. But don't forget to check with your parents first," said Sergeant Treadwell, a little more calmly. "I'm up at the mansion now. Mrs. von Buttermore will send her chauffeur to pick you up right away."

"No kidding? Awesome."

Mrs. von Buttermore was the richest person around. She lived in an enormous hilltop house built by her grandfather, a lumber baron. The only thing the grey-haired woman loved more than traveling all over the world was donating things to the Lakewood Hills community.

Hawkeye hung up and ran to his window. He picked up his flashlight and pointed it out into the dark, snowy night. He flashed it once, twice, three times. A second later, he got a response: three quick flashes of light from across the street. That meant Amy, who had been sitting at her desk doing her homework, would come right over.

Just after Hawkeye checked with his parents, Amy arrived at the front door, stomping snow from her bright blue boots. She wore a reddish parka that was about the same color as her hair.

"So what's going on?" she asked as she stepped in.

"A robbery at the von Buttermore mansion!"

Hawkeye quickly explained the situation. Fifteen minutes later, he and Amy were in the back seat of Mrs. von Buttermore's long, cream-colored limousine. The chauffeur, on the other side of a glass window, drove in silence.

"Boy, is this cool," said Hawkeye, admiring the woodwork inside.

Amy got up and walked to the television. "This car's enormous! And it even has a flat-screen TV."

The car passed through a pair of iron gates and started up the hill. At the end of the twisting drive, the lights of the von Buttermore mansion sparkled in the snowy night.

"Look at that house!" said Hawkeye. "I bet it has fifty rooms in it!"

"No way. Seventy-five rooms, at least." Amy's eyes opened wide.

When they reached the house, Mrs. von Buttermore opened the carved wooden front door herself.

"How good of you to come, Hawkeye and Amy. I'm Mrs. von Buttermore." She motioned behind her to a black and white Great Dane. "And this is my dog, Priceless. Do come in at once and get out of the cold."

She was a tall, lean woman with sharp features. For her dinner party, she was wearing an exotic gown that flowed to the floor.

As Hawkeye wiped his fogged-up glasses, Sergeant Treadwell came into the hallway. Amy didn't waste any time.

"Do you have any suspects yet, Sarge?" she asked.

"Yeah, can you tell us what happened?" said Hawkeye.

"Hold on. I've only had time to examine the scene of the crime." Sergeant Treadwell jotted something down in his notebook. "Mrs. von Buttermore was about to tell me all about it."

"Well, it's just awful." Her fingers twisted the rare Caribbean bead necklace that she was wearing. "I was having a dinner party for some old friends, and right while we were waiting for dinner to be served, someone broke into the library safe and stole the family jewels!"

"How many guests are there?" asked Sergeant Treadwell, taking notes.

"Six. We all chartered a yacht to explore some tropical islands a few years ago, and every so often we still get together."

Hawkeye said, "When were you last in the library before the robbery?"

Amy nodded. "Right, and when did you discover that the jewels had been stolen?"

"Well," said Mrs. von Buttermore, frowning slightly in concentration, "just before my friends came I put some diamonds and rubies into the safe. All the jewels were still there. Then we all chatted in the living room before dinner. Just before we went in to eat, I went into the library to get the map of our expedition. That's when I discovered that someone had broken into the safe and stolen all the jewels!"

"Let's see," said Hawkeye thoughtfully. "Did any of your guests leave the living room at any time?"

"Why, no. I'm sure none of them left." Mrs. von Buttermore shook her head. "And none of them would have stolen my jewels, if that's what you're thinking. For one thing, I don't think any of them need diamonds."

"Was anyone else here?" asked Amy.

"Yes, my two nephews, Toddy and Nicky, are visiting. They were listening to some CDs in the music room earlier this evening. Then Nicky went to the billiard room and stayed there the whole time. Toddy stayed in the music room and practiced the violin."

Hawkeye hesitated a moment before asking, "Is it possible that either one of them could have—"

"Heavens, no," interrupted Mrs. von Buttermore. In a whisper she said, "They're not my favorite relatives and they don't like each other at all, but neither one of them could have done it. First of all, Toddy was playing his violin the whole evening—I heard him. Secondly, to get into the library you have to go through the dining room, and they would have been seen."

Amy scratched her head. "But who would have seen them?"

"Ives, my butler. He would have seen them. He was in the dining room the whole time." Mrs. von Buttermore put her hand over her heart. "Oh, dear, I do hope he didn't do it. A good butler is so hard to find."

She shook her head. "No, he couldn't have done it. A maid was in the dining room with him. They were lighting the candles and whatnot."

"Well," said Sergeant Treadwell, "it looks like an outside job to me. When I checked the library, I noticed that one of the windows was open. Someone could have crawled in through the window, broken into the safe, and then escaped back out the window.

I think I'll check outside. There may be some tracks in the snow."

Hawkeye pulled out his sketch pad. "Hey, Sarge, I'll go with you."

"You guys go do that," said Amy, "and I'll take a look around in here."

Hawkeye and Sergeant Treadwell soon found what they were looking for. The tracks led clearly through the snow from a window of the billiard room to the library, and back again.

"Things don't look good for Nick," said Hawkeye. "He was the only one in the billiard room."

Hawkeye examined a few other things and then started to draw the footprints. He worked quickly, yet carefully. When he was sure that he had drawn them just the way they looked, he headed inside. Next, he drew a floor plan of the von Buttermore mansion.

"These footprints make it clear just who did it," Amy said.

When Mrs. von Buttermore saw the sketch, she said, "Why, Hawkeye, that's a marvelous drawing. Do you suppose that after all this is over, I could keep it as a souvenir of the evening?"

Hawkeye turned almost as red as Amy's hair and said, "Sure."

While Sergeant Treadwell talked with the dinner guests in the living room, Hawkeye and Amy sat down in the music room and examined the drawing.

"Well, I guess the butler didn't do it," said Amy, pointing to the tracks outside the library window.

Suddenly she snapped her fingers and elbowed Hawkeye in the ribs. "These footprints make it clear just who did it!"

WHO STOLE MRS. VON BUTTERMORE'S DIAMONDS?

The Mystery of the Helpful Professor

Hawkeye was huddled in the school library, reading about video games, when someone tapped his shoulder. He jumped in surprise.

"Psst, Hawkeye," whispered Rob, one of his friends from the soccer team. "Can I borrow a buck until tomorrow?"

A buck meant four quarters. Four quarters meant two tries at Hawkeye's favorite arcade game, the one with the crazy robots.

Hawkeye pulled a crumpled dollar bill from the pocket of his jeans. "This is all I have and I kind of had plans for it. You know, for a few games at the arcade."

"I really need to borrow a buck," pleaded Rob, looking both scared and nervous. "C'mon. You're the game champ already. Can't you take a break and lend me the buck? I really need it. I've got this huge spelling test next week. If I screw it up, I'll flunk the class."

Rob signaled Hawkeye to follow him. He led the way behind a shelf of books, and then pulled a sheet of paper from his spelling book.

"Some bald guy with glasses was passing these out in front of school this morning," whispered Rob. "It's an ad for a study guide, and I really need one."

He waved the piece of paper at Hawkeye. "Look. It says here on the back that Professor Newton— that's the guy's name—is a doctor of grammar from Harvard. I need the study guide right away so that I can have it in time to study for the spelling test."

Hawkeye took the piece of paper and read the message. He frowned.

"Forget this, Rob," he said, handing back the paper. "But you really are in trouble, aren't you? You'd better start studying for that exam right away or you'll never pass it."

WHAT WAS HAWKEYE TALKING ABOUT?

Dear Students,
  I know you have a big spelling test coming up. If you want to do well on the test, you must send for my especially helpfull study guide. Just send two dollars to my adress.
  Sincerelly,
  Proffesor Newton

Hawkeye took the piece of paper and read the message.

The Case of the
Daisy
Dispute

One windy day, Hawkeye and Amy were biking past Von Buttermore Park on their way to the arcade when they heard angry yelling. They jammed on their brakes and brought their bikes to a quick stop.

"Trouble," said Hawkeye.

"With a capital R," added Amy. "For Ratchet."

Mrs. Ratchet stood in her front yard yelling at a young blonde girl. Broom in hand, Mrs. Ratchet had the girl cornered in her garden. Hawkeye and Amy rode up to see what was going on.

"You were, too," shouted Mrs. Ratchet.

"Was not," responded the girl.

"Were, too."

"Was not."

"Hey," interrupted Hawkeye. "What's the deal? What happened?"

Mrs. Ratchet had the reputation of being the meanest person in Lakewood Hills. She always had a broom in hand, and if any dogs, cats, or kids dared step on her property, she chased after them, screaming and waving it at them.

Mrs. Ratchet brushed her hair away from her face and turned to Hawkeye and Amy.

"None of your business," said Mrs. Ratchet. "And what are you two doing on my property?"

"We heard all this yelling," said Hawkeye.

Amy put down her bike. "Yeah, so we came to see if someone needed help."

"I... I need help," said the girl, her voice shaking.

Mrs. Ratchet turned to the girl and threatened her with the end of the broom. "No, you don't. You need to tell the truth. You need to admit that you were stealing daisies out of my garden."

"Was not."

"Were, too."

With big, innocent eyes, the girl looked at Hawkeye and Amy. "Honest, I wasn't. I was sitting over in the park on that bench. I was reading my book of poetry and a huge gust of wind came up and blew my papers away. I chased them, but they blew all the way across the street and into Mrs. Ratchet's flower bed."

A nasty scowl on her face, Mrs. Ratchet said, "Oh, baloney!"

The girl thrust out a handful of papers. "See, here are my things."

"Well, what's that in your other hand, a goldfish or something?" asked Mrs. Ratchet, smiling a little at her snide joke.

"No, Mrs. Ratchet. They're flowers. Your flowers," said the girl as she held up a handful of daisies. "I'm sorry, but I broke them off when I was getting my things. I was going to bring them to you."

"Oh, you were not!"

"Was, too."

There was no stopping them. Mrs. Ratchet, certain that the girl was guilty, started yelling and shaking her broom again. The girl continued to plead her innocence.

Amy rolled her eyes at Hawkeye. "This could go on all day. I wonder who's telling the truth."

"I've got a hunch."

Mrs. Ratchet stood in her front yard, yelling at a young blonde girl.

Hawkeye took out his sketch pad and pencil. He did a drawing of the park and of Mrs. Ratchet's house and yard. When he finished, he held out the drawing to Amy.

"My hunch was right," whispered Hawkeye. "Now what?"

"Beats me," said Amy. "I don't think they'll stop to let us explain!"

WHO WAS RIGHT ABOUT WHAT HAD HAPPENED, MRS. RATCHET OR THE GIRL?

The Case of the
Bouncing
Check

With some of the reward money they had gotten from Mrs. von Buttermore, Hawkeye and Amy went to The Eatery for a lunch of burgers and fries. One of the older restaurants in town, it had been renovated recently and drew a crowd of both old and new customers.

From their table, Amy looked around. Every seat was filled and the front windows were all steamed up. It seemed as if all the people in the restaurant were talking as loudly as they could.

"As my mom says, this joint's jumping." Amy thought of her food and smacked her lips. "I hope our order comes soon. I just love French fries.

There'd better be a ton of 'em— with lots of ketchup. Yum. I love, love, love them."

Hawkeye stopped playing with the salt and pepper shakers and shook his head. "Amy, you love everything."

"That's not true." Amy tapped her head and thought for a moment. "I hate fingernails dragged across a blackboard, game remotes that stick, and... and... I know, I hate broccoli and that pepperoni that you always order on your half of the pizza."

"Mmm, pepperoni." Hawkeye's eyes lit up. "Now, there's something I love. I love—"

He was cut off by an angry woman shouting at a waitress. The woman, seated right behind Hawkeye, was fairly plump and wore a fake leopard-skin jacket.

"What?" said the woman loudly, snapping her checkbook shut. She was disgusted. "What do you mean, you won't accept my check without identification?" The woman snorted and arranged the blue hair piled high on her head. "Young woman, you have deeply insulted me."

"I'm sorry, ma'am." The waitress turned the color of ketchup. "But that's the manager's policy. Don't you have a driver's license or something?"

The woman raised her shrill voice even louder, so that everyone in the restaurant could hear. "My chauffeur is the one with the license. My check is quite good, I assure you. Now, my dear, I'm late to see Jean." The woman turned to her friend seated next to her. "Isn't that right, Muffy?"

"Oh, absolutely, Babs. We simply must run."

Hawkeye leaned over to Amy. "And some people complain about *kids* in restaurants! I wouldn't trust that woman as far as I could throw her."

"Please don't try, Hawkeye," said Amy, rolling her eyes.

"I'd be happy to have you speak to the manager, but he's not here," said the waitress. "Perhaps one of your friends has some identification I could see."

The woman was furious. "How terrible! They're my guests, it is my check, and you want to bother them?"

The woman stood up, put her hands on her hips, and glared at the waitress. "My dear, either you accept my check or you call the police and have them take me to jail. Really, I've never seen service like this before!"

Suddenly the noisy restaurant became absolutely quiet, as every single customer turned to see what the racket was all about. Realizing that everyone was watching her, the waitress was too embarrassed to speak. Only the sound of sizzling burgers and fries filled the air.

Her voice shaking, the waitress finally said, "I... I guess I'll take your check. I just wish my boss were here."

Muttering nasty words, the loud woman and her four friends marched out of the restaurant. Two minutes later, the manager returned and the waitress rushed over to show him the check.

"Why, that check's no good!" he groaned. "I just came from the bank and they warned me not to accept a check from that woman. The name on the check is false, the address is false, and there is no money in that bank account. She's been bouncing checks all over town."

The waitress began to protest. "Yes, but I..."

"I gave you strict instructions not to take a check without identification." The manager shook his head. "I'm sorry, but you're going to have to pay that woman's bill. And that might not be the least of your problems."

A few minutes later, the waitress brought Hawkeye and Amy their order.

"Wow, I'm in such trouble," said the waitress, her eyes red. "The manager's so mad he might even fire me."

"Come on, Amy." Hawkeye got up and took out his sketch pad. "Let's see if we can help. There have to be some clues on the table. Maybe we can find out where she went."

"Yeah, we'll find that nasty woman for you," said Amy to the waitress. "Just bring me the ketchup and don't worry about anything else."

They walked over to the table. "What a mess they left," Amy sniffed.

While Hawkeye sketched, Amy examined the clues.

"Hey," she said suddenly, "I know where we—"

"—can find that woman," Hawkeye finished with a grin. "Let's get going!"

"There have to be some clues on the table," Hawkeye said.

WHERE DID HAWKEYE AND AMY FIND THE WOMAN?

The Mystery of the
Hardware
Heist

Hawkeye glanced up at the clock in the bookstore window as he and Amy walked by, jingling quarters in their pockets.

"It's 3:30, Amy," Hawkeye said. "That means we can get in a couple of hours at the arcade."

Amy motioned toward Nosey, who had followed them. "What about Nosey?"

"Oh, I guess we should take her home. Let's go."

As they rounded the corner, they saw the flashing red lights of Sergeant Treadwell's squad car.

"Hey, let's see what's up!" said Amy, racing off. "Definitely."

Bounding alongside Nosey, they ran up to see what had happened. Sergeant Treadwell and Rosa Garcia, the manager of the Nuts & Bolts Hardware, stood on the sidewalk, along with several other people. Nosey pushed through the group and nudged Sergeant Treadwell.

"I'm glad to see you two here," he said. "And you, too, Nosey. There's been a robbery."

"Wow! What happened?" asked Hawkeye.

Rosa, who was quite nervous, talked quickly, drawing pictures in the air with her hands. "I went into the back room to pour myself another cup of coffee. When I came out, there was this man taking money out of the cash register and stuffing it into his pockets."

Amy's eyes opened wide. "Really? What did you do?"

"I was so mad I couldn't even scream." Rosa smiled. "So I picked up a can of car wax and threw it at him as hard as I could. Hit him, too, but he didn't stop. He ran out of the store and into the park across the street. I chased him, but he was too fast for me."

Sergeant Treadwell frowned as he wrote all this down. "Lucky for you he didn't have a weapon."

Hawkeye asked, "Did you get a look at him?"

"Yeah," said Amy, nodding, "can you tell us what he was wearing?"

"Well, he was wearing a dark raincoat and *that*." Rosa pointed to a black and red ski mask lying on the sidewalk. "He must have taken it off and dropped it as he ran away. He was wearing it in the store, so I didn't see his face at all."

"That's too bad." Sergeant Treadwell stopped writing and thought for a moment. "It's going to be tough finding the thief."

"Well, you've got to find him," said Rosa, shaking the ski mask at the sergeant. "You can't have a robber on the loose. He only got away with a couple of bucks from the register, but it's terrible. Sergeant, you have to find him."

"You're right, but how? The only clue we have is this ski mask."

Out of the corner of her eye, Amy noticed Nosey delicately sniffing a fire hydrant.

"I know," she said, smiling. "We'll let Nosey smell the ski mask."

"Great idea, Amy," said Hawkeye. "Then, maybe she'll lead the way to the suspect!"

"Oh, Amy!" said Rosa, pleased with the idea. "We must catch him and put a stop to this sort of thing."

Hawkeye called out to his dog, "Come here, Nosey!"

He took the ski mask and held it up to Nosey. The dog, wagging her tail, sniffed it.

"Take a good whiff," said Hawkeye. "Okay, now *find*, Nosey, *find* the person who wore this mask. Go on, *find* him."

The dog glanced up at Hawkeye and barked, then put her nose to the ground. In an instant she was off, bounding across the street and into Von Buttermore Park. Some men who had been cutting the grass before it rained watched as Hawkeye, Amy, and Sergeant Treadwell chased after the dog. Rosa stayed behind and tried to count the cash that was left in the cash register so she would know how much had been taken.

Nosey made her way past a statue of Mrs. von Buttermore's great-grandfather, the Civil War hero, seated on his horse, and continued around a fountain and out the other side of the park. With Amy in the lead, Hawkeye following close behind, and Sergeant Treadwell a distant third, Nosey led the group to a pleasant yellow house.

A friendly looking young man in his early twenties was just coming out of it. Nosey jumped up and licked him in the face.

"Oh, gross!" said the man, pushing Nosey away.

Amy and Hawkeye hurried up to him.

"This... this... isn't your ski mask, is it?" asked Hawkeye, slightly out of breath.

The young man appeared surprised. "No. No, of course not. It's not even winter. What would I be doing with a ski mask? Get this dog away from me."

"Nosey, come here," called Hawkeye.

Sergeant Treadwell, huffing and puffing, finally arrived. He tried desperately to catch his breath, while he mopped his face with a bright red bandana.

"Have... have you... you," he panted, "been home this afternoon?"

"Yes. All afternoon." The young man was rather annoyed. "I've been inside watching television all day. I just finished watching *The Good Old Days* a few minutes ago. Now I'm on my way to work. I work nights."

The sergeant shoved the bandana back in his pocket and then continued with his questions. Nosey spotted a squirrel and took off around the side of the house.

"Nosey," called Amy, "come here! Come back here!"

Hawkeye frowned. Something wasn't right about the young man's story.

"Um, I'll go get her," he said.

This was the moment Hawkeye had been waiting for, and he jogged after his dog. He slipped around the corner of the house and found Nosey at the base of a tree.

"Hey, Nosey, what's going on?" he asked. "Your nose wouldn't lie to you, would it? You think that guy was the masked bandit, don't you, girl?"

Hawkeye took a couple of quick steps over to the house. Standing on his tiptoes, he peered through a large window and into the young man's living room.

"You bet there's something wrong here. That guy's story is as phony as a three-dollar bill," he said to himself. "Sarge better see this."

Hawkeye whipped out his sketch pad and pencil and did a hasty drawing. He paused, squinted as he studied the living room, and then added some more details. When he was sure he had gotten everything, Hawkeye took Nosey by the collar and returned to the front of the house.

"Well, sounds like you're pretty clear to me," Sergeant Treadwell was saying to the young man. "Sorry to disturb you. I've got your number here, so if I have any more questions I'll give you a call."

"Yep," said the young man, who turned and started to walk off.

Hawkeye hurried over to Amy, showed her the drawing, and whispered in her ear.

"Hawkeye, you're right!" she gasped. "Hey, Sarge, look at this!"

They quickly showed Sergeant Treadwell the drawing.

"Uh-oh," said the sergeant. He called out, "Ah, young man! Could you hang on there for a moment? I've got a few more questions for you, after all."

Standing on his tiptoes, Hawkeye peered through a large window into the young man's living room.

WHAT DID HAWKEYE SEE THAT CONVINCED SERGEANT TREADWELL TO ASK MORE QUESTIONS?

The Case of
Lucy's Lost
Lemonade

After a late afternoon meeting of their computer club, Hawkeye and Amy stuffed their books into their backpacks and headed home.

As they came out the large doors of Lakewood Hills Elementary and into the warm afternoon air, they heard angry shouting from the soccer field. A six-year-old blonde girl with no front teeth was yelling as loudly as she could.

"Hey, that's my sister, Lucy!" shouted Amy, bursting into a run.

The Lakewood Loons fourth-grade soccer team had just finished playing a game against another school. Hawkeye cut through the crowd and hurried after Amy. Seconds later, he and Amy reached Lucy and her lemonade stand.

"You big bulli*th*!"" shouted Lucy angrily. She unleashed her lethargic Saint Bernard. "Get 'em, Bernie! Go on, get those creep*th*!"

The big, sleepy dog managed to clamber to his feet and let out a couple of enormous barks. Frightened, a boy and girl backed up against a tree. The dog barked playfully and trotted over to them.

"Hey, call off your dog!" shouted the boy, who was still wearing his soccer uniform. He waved his muddy hands. "I didn't drink your lemonade, kid. Get your dog out of here!"

"It wasn't me, either. I didn't drink your lemonade. Just get that dog away from me!" pleaded the girl, waving her pom poms. She had been selling raffle tickets at the soccer game and was dressed in a yellow and orange clown outfit.

Amy said, "Lucy, what in the heck's going on? And what's Bernie doing at school? Call him back."

"No way." Lucy, a little short for her age but pretty tough, put her hands on her hips. She clenched her teeth and the tip of her tongue stuck out in the space where teeth should have been. "I'm not calling Bernie back until they tell me who drank all my lemonade. They have to pay for it."

Hawkeye glanced to his left and checked out the lemonade stand. A large, empty plastic pitcher stood on it.

"You mean someone drank all that?" he asked.

"Ye*th*. One of 'em did." Lucy pointed to the soccer player and the clown. "I've been here at the *th*tand making lemonade for people from the *th*occer game. When I went in for more cup*th*, I had more than half a pitcher left. Then, when I came back, I found the pitcher on the ground, completely empty. And these two were out here. One of them ha*th* to pay for it!"

Bernie saw Hawkeye and Amy and wandered over to greet them. The boy in the soccer uniform heaved a sigh of relief. The girl in the clown outfit, a big smile painted on her face, smiled even more.

"Lucy's right," said Amy. "If you guys drank it, you have to pay for it."

"I swear I didn't drink it," said the boy, chewing his gum. "I was just walking home from the soccer game. I didn't go anywhere near her silly old lemonade stand. It must have been her." He pointed to the clown.

The girl opened her eyes wide. "Me? It wasn't me. I didn't go near the stand, either. I promise you, I didn't touch the lemonade."

"*Th*omebody's got to pay for it and it'*th* not going to be me," Lucy stated flatly. "I wanted to make *th*ome money. One of you ha*th* to pay."

Amy gave a big sisterly shrug and said, "Lay off, Lucy. Wait a minute." She turned to Hawkeye. "Let's do a little sleuthing, Hawkeye."

Hawkeye grinned, set his backpack on the ground, and took his sketch pad from his back pocket.

"A quick sketch should take care of this one," he said. "The place is littered with clues."

"Yeah." Amy was already examining the footprints around the lemonade stand. "These tracks should tell us something."

Hawkeye studied the scene for a moment, bit his lip, and then started to draw.

"Hey, look," he said, his hand sketching quickly, "there's a clue on the stand, too."

While Hawkeye and Amy tried to figure out what had happened, Lucy, the soccer player, and the clown all started arguing again. Bernie wagged his tail and happily picked up his barking.

A few short minutes later, Amy shouted out above the ruckus, "Hey, you guys, cool it! Hawkeye and I have got it figured out."

Lucy fell silent and her mouth dropped open. "Are you kidding me?"

"No joke, Lucy," said Hawkeye. He handed her the drawing. "Neither one of these two is telling the truth, but only one of them drank the lemonade. Let's see how good you are at mysteries."

"I didn't drink your lemonade," cried the girl.

WHO DRANK LUCY'S LEMONADE?

The Mystery of the
Missing
Money

"Dad," said Hawkeye as they rode in their small station wagon, "a kid at school says that when you sneeze, the air comes rushing out of your body at a hundred miles an hour."

Mr. Collins laughed. "Really? Where'd he pick that up?"

"In a movie or something. Do you think it's true?"

"Could be. Next time you sneeze, I'll clock it."

Mr. Collins turned into the driveway of a tan, split-level house. He brought the car to a stop and shut off the ignition.

"Well, here we are," he said. "You want to come in with me? It shouldn't take too long. I just have to run in and pick up some money for one of my clients. He's been waiting a long time for this payment."

"Sure, I'll come."

Hawkeye climbed out of the car and followed his father up to the house. A few rooms were lit up, and the front door was partway open.

"Mr. Turner's expecting me," said Mr. Collins when he noticed the open front door. He knocked several times. "Hello? Anybody home?"

There was no answer. They stuck their heads in and heard some faint groaning from inside the house.

"Ohhh, ohhh..."

"Mr. Turner?" called Mr. Collins. "Mr. Turner?"

"Ohhh, ohhh..."

Hawkeye pointed across the room. "In there, Dad!"

Hawkeye and his father rushed over to Mr. Turner. Moaning and groaning, Mr. Turner was lying on the floor in front of a long bar. On the floor beside him was an empty briefcase.

"Wh... what happened," mumbled Mr. Turner.

Hawkeye said excitedly, "We just got here and you were lying on the floor."

Mr. Turner rubbed the top of his head. "Someone must have sneaked up behind me and bopped me on the head. Ow."

Mr. Collins wasn't sure what to think. "Why would someone do something like that?"

"My gosh!" gasped Mr. Turner, pointing to the empty briefcase that lay on the floor. "My briefcase... it was full of the money I was supposed to give you. Someone must have stolen it!"

"You're kidding." Hawkeye looked concerned.

"No, I'm not kidding," said Mr. Turner, anger flashing in his eyes. He turned to Mr. Collins.

"I'd just paid the plumber, who had come to fix my sink. I saw him out the door and then went over to the bar and poured myself a glass of soda water. Someone knocked. I thought it was you. I called out and told you—at least, I thought it was you—to come in. I heard a few steps behind me, and I was about to turn and greet you. That's the last thing I remember."

"So you're saying someone must have knocked you on the head and stolen the money," said Hawkeye.

"Sonny, that's exactly how it must have happened." Mr. Turner shook his head. "Oh, this is terrible."

Mr. Collins glanced over at Hawkeye and winked. Then, his right hand in the air, he pretended he was drawing.

Hawkeye got it. Pretending to be bored, he wandered over to a chair at the side of the room. He sat down and polished his glasses. Gradually, so as not to attract attention, he took out his sketch pad.

Mr. Collins turned to Mr. Turner. His voice flat, he said, "You realize, of course, that you're still liable. My client will expect you to pay him the money you owe him just as soon as possible. I certainly hope you have some insurance to cover this theft."

Hawkeye paid careful attention to the bar where Mr. Turner said he had been standing. He quickly sketched in the shelves, the mirror behind the bar, and the wall, and then concentrated on finding any clues.

A moment later, Hawkeye grinned. He'd done it again. When Mr. Turner went into the kitchen to put some ice on his head, Hawkeye called his father aside.

"Dad," whispered Hawkeye, "here's the evidence."

Mr. Collins examined the drawing. "Good going, Hawkeye. You broke the case. Let's show this to Mr. Turner."

WHO STOLE MR. TURNER'S MONEY?

"I went over to the bar and poured myself
a glass of soda water," Mr. Turner said.

The Case of the
Bashed
Boss

On their way to Von Buttermore Park, Amy kidded Hawkeye about his t-shirt.

"But, Amy," said Hawkeye, examining his chest, "I don't care if this spaceship is—"

Just as they passed the 55 Flavors Ice Cream Store, they heard a distant cry.

"Help! Help! Someone call an ambulance!"

Amy gasped. "Wow! Come on, Hawkeye," she said as she broke into a run. "Someone needs help!"

Amy swung open the door of the store, and she and Hawkeye hurried in. But there was no one in the store. A dish of chocolate fudge ice cream sat melting on a table, a sliced banana lay on the counter, and the snow cone machine whirled on and on, spitting out a growing mound of ice shavings.

"Really weird," said Hawkeye, glancing about.

"Someone's got to be around somewhere." Amy scratched her head. "I mean, that split banana was about to become a banana split."

Then the cry came again.

"Someone call an ambulance! Call the police!"

"Quick, the basement!" said Hawkeye, pulling out his sketch pad as he hurried to the back of the store.

Wasting no time, he and Amy ran down the stairs, past stacks of supplies, and into a small basement office.

A woman customer and two store employees, Bertha and Joe, were bent over the store owner, Mr. Hardy. Dressed in an old black suit, he laid face down and unconscious. There was no blood, but a bump on the back of his head had swollen to the size of a goose egg.

"I'll call Sergeant Treadwell and an ambulance!" Amy rushed out of the room and back upstairs.

"Will he be all right?" asked Hawkeye. "What happened?"

"Yeah, he'll be fine," said Bertha with a wave of her hand.

"I came down here for more change," said Joe, "and I found Mr. Hardy right here on the floor, out cold."

The woman customer shook her head. "You know, it's no wonder this happened. Even I know that Mr. Hardy is the meanest store owner in town—and the stingiest, too."

Mr. Hardy started to wake up. "Oh, oh, my head..."

"Looks like he'll be back to his old self in no time," said Joe, wiping his nose with his sleeve.

Bertha groaned. "Lucky us."

Slightly out of breath, Amy came back down. "The ambulance will be right here."

"Well, why aren't they here right now?" said Mr. Hardy crossly, as he sat up. "Joe, darn you, give me a hand! And Bertha, quit being so lazy! Come over here on the other side. Hurry, blast it all!"

Mr. Hardy muttered and complained and cursed nonstop. By the time they got him upstairs, Sergeant Treadwell and an ambulance had arrived.

"What took you so long?" yelled Mr. Hardy.

As the ambulance attendants carried him outside and loaded him into the ambulance, the cot he was lying on bumped into the door.

"Not so rough, you ninnies! What a bunch of fumbling idiots!" He reached into his old coat pocket. "Blast. Where's my wallet? I had fifty dollars in it. My wallet, my wallet..."

His shouting could be heard until the attendants closed the back doors of the ambulance and drove away.

When they were gone, Sergeant Treadwell heaved a sigh of relief. "Whew. Now, what happened here?"

He turned to Hawkeye. "You've got sharp eyes. Did you see anything?"

"Not much, Sarge," said Hawkeye, shrugging. "But it looks like someone went down to the basement, snuck into Mr. Hardy's office, and knocked him out." Hawkeye had seen something unusual, but he wasn't going to let on until he and Amy had questioned the suspects.

Amy turned to the woman customer and the two employees, who were seated at a table. She asked, "Who went downstairs besides Joe?"

Joe rubbed his chin. "Hey, listen, I just went down to get change. You know, the safe's in Mr. Hardy's office." He thought for a second. "Bertha went down, too."

Bertha, scowling, became defensive. "I went to get syrup for the snow cone machine. But that was over an hour ago, and I didn't even go into Mr. Hardy's office. This customer went downstairs after I did."

The woman choked on her words. "M-m-me? I just went to the bathroom a few minutes ago. That was all. I swear."

"So, any of you could have done it." Sergeant Treadwell made some notes in a small notebook. "What was Mr. Hardy hit with?"

Amy tugged on her red pigtail. "I didn't see anything, Sarge. Did you, Hawkeye?"

"Nope."

Sergeant Treadwell continued questioning the three suspects. Hawkeye leaned over to Amy.

"If we can figure out how it happened," he whispered, "then maybe that'll tell us who hit Mr. Hardy—and why. I want to take a look at something down there."

"Me, too."

Together, Hawkeye and Amy slipped out of the group and ran downstairs. They stood in the doorway, staring into Mr. Hardy's office.

"Something's odd here," said Hawkeye, focusing on one thing, then another.

Amy looked at him. "Well, let's try to find out what was used for a weapon." She nudged him. "Do a sketch, Hawkeye. Maybe that'll turn up something."

"Right."

He studied the office for a moment, then set pencil to paper. He was careful to include every detail.

"Don't forget the stuff on the desk," said Amy.

When the drawing was complete, the two of them examined it. Hawkeye snapped his fingers.

"Look, Amy!"

"You bet," she agreed. Quickly, she yelled upstairs, "Hey, Sarge, don't let anyone up there leave. One of them did it and we know how... and who!"

WHO ATTACKED MR. HARDY?
HOW WAS IT DONE?

Hawkeye said, "If we can figure out how it happened,
then maybe we'll know who hit Mr. Hardy—and why."

The Secret of the Ancient Treasure

Part 1
The Black Cave

On a warm, sunny, spring afternoon, Hawkeye and
Amy borrowed a couple of dirt bikes and rode down
Old Mill Creek Road. Nosey, her nose high and
her tongue hanging out, charged along faster than
Hawkeye and Amy could ride. The road was an old
muddy track filled with potholes.

"This road is great," said Hawkeye, zigzagging among the water-filled holes. "It's kind of like a slalom course."

"I'll say!"

"Come on," said Hawkeye over his shoulder. "We'd better hurry up and get to the caves before it gets much later."

Without replying, Amy leaned over her handlebars and sped right past Hawkeye.

The low bluffs along Mill Creek were famous for their caverns and tunnels, which were rumored to have once been the secret hideouts of bandits and gangs.

"There it is!" said Amy, pointing to one of the caves. "That's the cave where Matt Chang found the fossils—right beside an underground river."

They rode up to the cave, Nosey just ahead of them. At the mouth of the cavern, they stopped, laid down their dirt bikes, and peered into the black opening.

"This place is sort of creepy," said Amy.

Hawkeye nodded. "I'll say." He took a flashlight from his pocket and aimed it inside the cave. "You know, we really don't have to go in. But I sure want to find some fossils and see that underground river!"

"Count me in," said Amy, her green eyes sparkling. "I can't imagine what it's like."

Amy took a ball of kite string from her pocket and said, "We're going to do just like Tom Sawyer, Hawkeye. I'm going to tie this kite string to my bike, and unroll it as we go in. I mean, I want to be able to get out of there!"

"Definitely," said Hawkeye. He started looking around for Nosey. "Boy, if my parents find out about this, I'm going to be grounded for the rest of my life."

Hawkeye called Nosey over and took the dog by the collar. Together the trio set off into the caves, and the bright spring day dissolved behind them.

As Hawkeye led the way with the beam of his flashlight, Amy let out the kite string behind them. The first room was large and fairly dry. At the other end, it split into two small tunnels.

Nosey was the bravest of the three, her nose down on the ground, sniffing eagerly. Hawkeye held her tightly by the collar so that she wouldn't run off.

They followed the tunnel to the left. With the opening now out of sight, it was much darker, and the passage seemed to lead downward.

"This is creep city," said Hawkeye as the passage narrowed.

"Definitely. Look at the walls—there's water dripping down all over."

The tunnel forked, and, following Matt's directions, they took the left branch, shuffling their feet. Gradually, they began to hear something.

"That sounds like... like a..." Amy cupped her ear.

"A river," said Hawkeye, smiling for the first time.

Some ten feet further on, they came to an opening and turned right. The bubbling sound of running water filled their ears. They entered another room, its ceiling arching high overhead, and by the beam of the flashlight they saw it: an underground river. The rushing water looked murky in the gloomy light.

Hawkeye let go of Nosey and hurried forward to the edge.

"Oh, man," he breathed, sweeping the light across the water.

Amy came up beside him. "I wonder if it has a bottom. You can't see a thing below the surface."

Just then, Nosey trotted up behind Amy and bumped the back of her legs. Her knees buckled forward and she fell into the stream, screaming and splashing.

"Help, Hawkeye!"

Hawkeye grabbed her hand and pulled as hard as he could. The flashlight beam bounced wildly around the walls of the cavern. Nosey barked with excitement, her voice echoing crazily in the chamber.

Amy struggled to her feet and climbed out, dripping wet. "Oooh, that water's icy. Thanks for grabbing me. I thought it would be over my head, but it's only about a foot-and-a-half deep—here, at least." She wrung water out of her sweatshirt sleeve.

Nosey, still excited, plunged into the water and bounded across to the other side.

"Look at that!" yelled Hawkeye. "It's shallow all the way across. And look at that rock ledge—it's perfect for fossils. Let's go!"

He stepped into the water, feeling the way with the toes of his running shoes. Amy followed him in. When they reached the other side, they scrambled up the slippery bank and began to search for fossils in the damp gravel.

As Hawkeye shined the flashlight around them, its beam glinted off something buried in the gravel nearby.

"Hey, Amy, this is weird. There's something buried here. It looks like part of a metal box." He started brushing away some dirt.

"Nosey," he called. "Come on over here. Come on over here and dig. Dig, Nosey, dig."

Nosey trotted over and began to dig furiously where Hawkeye had pointed. Soon the dog figured out that there really was something buried, and she couldn't stop. Her paws cut through the gravel, and a minute later she uncovered a battered metal box.

Hawkeye bent over and picked it up. Amy whispered, "Wow. Maybe there's a treasure inside."

Leaning over Hawkeye's shoulder, she said, "Look, there's a latch!"

"Here, take this," Hawkeye said, handing her the flashlight.

Fumbling with excitement, Hawkeye set the box on the ground and reached for the rusty metal latch.

He glanced up at Amy. "Well, here goes."

He struggled with the latch for a moment and then flipped it. Then he took hold of the lid and forced it open. Inside was an old piece of thick paper, yellowed and torn around the edges. On it was a drawing.

Hawkeye carefully lifted the paper out of the box. Amy brought the flashlight down close.

"It's a map!" exclaimed Hawkeye.

Amy's eyes opened wide. "Well, it's not buried treasure, but maybe it's a treasure map."

Hawkeye carefully studied the map. He noted the initials at the top and at the bottom, but was confused by what appeared to be a code.

"Hawkeye, you know what this looks like?" said Amy, pointing to the right-hand side of the map. "It looks kind of like a lake. And this... this looks like a—"

"A river!" Hawkeye slapped his forehead. "Mill Creek! Wow—maybe this is the route to some treasure!"

"And that square up there would be Mrs. von Buttermore's estate." Amy whistled in astonishment. "Hawkeye, this is some kind of map leading from the eaves to Mrs. von Buttermore's mansion."

"Yeah, but look at this crazy route shooting up and down," said Hawkeye, scratching his head. "What could such a crooked route mean? And what about all these letters and numbers?"

Amy thought for a moment. "Maybe the route leads to different places first—and there's something at each place—and then it goes to Mrs. von Buttermore's."

"Yeah..." Hawkeye shut the box. "Come on, let's go outside and take a look. Maybe we can figure out where it goes."

He carefully put the map back in the box and tucked it under his arm. Then he grabbed Nosey by the collar. Excited, they quickly crossed the stream and picked up the string.

Flashlight in hand, Amy led the way out, rewinding the string as they went. When they reached the outside, they had to shield their eyes from the bright light.

"That sun didn't seem this bright before," said Amy, squinting.

Hawkeye covered his eyes and let go of Nosey, who bounded off into a field. Then Hawkeye made his way over to a large boulder and spread the map out on it. When his eyes finally adjusted to the daylight, he started going over the map again. Amy tossed the string over by the dirt bikes and came over.

"If these little zigzags lead somewhere," he said, "the first one ought to lead down there."

Hawkeye pointed down the bluff and across the creek. On the other side of the stream was a wide-open field.

Amy checked the map, looked at the field in the distance, and frowned. She turned around and looked up the side of the steep bluff.

"Yeah, but then the next one would lead up there," she said, pointing upward. "And that's impossible. Nobody could climb up there."

"Nope." Hawkeye, scrunching up his forehead, returned to the map and studied it. "Hey, maybe these numbers and letters tell you how far to go in each direction. Maybe it's some kind of code or... or..."

Amy thought of something, snapped her fingers, and jabbed Hawkeye's side.

"That's exactly what it is, Hawkeye!" she said. "I saw something like this in one of Lucy's code books. All these numbers and letters tell you where to go!"

Muttering to herself, she pointed to one thing on the map, then another. With her finger, she traced the arrow from beginning to end.

"Got it!" she finally said, a big smile on her face. "I broke the code—I know where the map leads!"

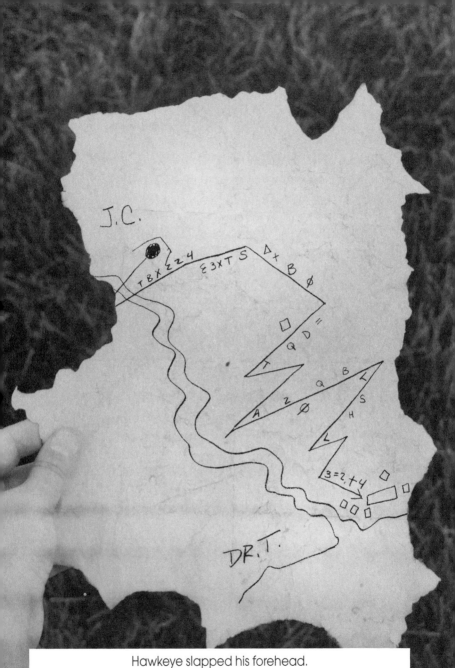

Hawkeye slapped his forehead.
"Wow—maybe this is the route to some treasure!"

WHERE DID THE SECRET MAP LEAD?

For the solution to this story and more of "The Secret of the Ancient Treasure" see *The Case of the Chocolate Snatcher*, Volume 2 in the **Can You Solve the Mystery?**™series.

Solution

The Secret of the
Long-Lost Cousin

Hawkeye noticed that his grandmother was the baby in the picture. But Dan had said that Hawkeye's grandmother was the "older sister." When Hawkeye asked him about this at dinner the next night, Dan suddenly remembered an urgent meeting and dashed out of the house.

Police stopped him as he tried to return the rental car at the airport. He admitted that he had been released from prison recently in Alaska, where he had been a cellmate of the real Cousin Dan. While he had been there, the man had heard all about Dan's family.

"I came here to trick the Collins family into a shady investment scheme, but I hadn't reckoned on Chrisopher—I mean, Hawkeye. He's one smart kid," he said.

Because he hadn't actually committed a crime, the man was released and never heard from again.

Solution

The Case of the
Disappearing Diamonds

The obvious suspect was, of course, Nicky von Buttermore. As shown by the tracks, he could have crawled out the billiard room window, run through the snow, and climbed in the library window. But a real thief would try not to leave such clear prints. Amy noticed that the prints leading from the library were made first because they were beneath the tracks coming from the billiard room.

"That means someone was trying to make it look like Nicky stole the diamonds," said Amy. "But there was another way into the library without being seen. And the person who could have entered it that way was Toddy."

When Sergeant Treadwell questioned Toddy, he confessed that he had stolen the diamonds. He had put on a CD of violin music, then snuck out the music room window and around the house to the library. "I wasn't going to keep the diamonds," he whined, "I only did it so Auntie dear would like me more than Nicky."

Solution

The Mystery of the
Helpful Professor

The letter couldn't have come from a qualified professor because it was so poorly written. Hawkeye found several mistakes (helpful, address, Sincerely, Professor).

"A person who made that many mistakes," said Hawkeye, "couldn't know much about spelling. This Professor Newton is a phony. Save your money, Rob, because you already have a great study guide—this letter."

Instead of sending in two dollars, Rob corrected the letter and returned it to Professor Newton, who was never heard from again. Hawkeye gave Rob some other tips on spelling. For a break later, the two of them went to the arcade, and they both got their names on the screen.

"If you can do that well on a game," said Hawkeye, "I'm sure you can do great on the spelling test!"

Solution

The Case of the
Daisy Dispute

The girl said that she had chased after the papers when a gust of wind came up and blew them from the park and into Mrs. Rachet's garden. From the trees in Hawkeye's drawing, you can tell which direction the wind was blowing.

"It's blowing from the house toward the park," said Hawkeye. "The girl's lying because there's no way the wind could have carried her papers into the garden."

When Hawkeye and Amy started to interrupt the unending argument, Mrs. Rachet spun around and told them to get off her property.

"Well, we tried," said Hawkeye as they got on their bikes and rode away.

"Yeah," said Amy. "If Mrs. Rachet wouldn't listen, too bad for her. I think the girl had already been punished enough!"

Solution

The Case of the
Bouncing Check

The woman and her friends left a few things on the table that gave clues about them. The bus transfers indicated that they had all come by bus and that the woman didn't have a chauffeur at all. And the ticket from the pawnshop showed that she wasn't as wealthy as she had pretended to be.

But the main clue was the torn matchbook by her plate. Amy saw the letters and remembered that the woman had said that she was late to see Jean. Amy figured that the matchbook was from Jean-Pierre's Hair Design, a beauty shop.

Sure enough, at two o'clock the woman, Babs Morgan, showed up at Jean-Pierre's. But rather than a haircut, she got a free ride to the police station from Sergeant Treadwell.

The waitress was so relieved and thankful that she treated Hawkeye and Amy to an enormous batch of French fries.

Solution

The Mystery of the
Hardware
Heist

The young man said that he had just finished watching *The Good Old Days* on TV. That program finished at 2:30, however, according to the TV guide, and it was a little past 3:30 when Sergeant Treadwell had spoken to him.

Amy added, "He might not be the guy who robbed the *Nuts & Bolts Hardware*, but he sure hasn't been home all afternoon."

The young man claimed that he had recorded the program on his DVR, but police later matched his fingerprints with some that had been found on the cash register, and he was arrested.

Sergeant Treadwell made Nosey an honorary police dog and bought her a big, squeaky chew toy.

Solution

The Case of
Lucy's Lost Lemonade

Both the soccer player and the clown stopped by the stand, shown by the footprints (his cleats and her large clown shoes). The girl came first, because the boy stepped on some strands from her pom poms with his cleats, making holes in them.

Lucy spotted the boy's tracks leading to the pitcher, but she didn't notice that his dirty finger-prints were only on the stand.

"There's clown lipstick on the pitcher, though," said Amy. "And that means—"

The girl cut Amy off, claiming that if she hadn't gotten there first and drank Lucy's lemonade, the soccer player would have. Her big clown smile turned to a frown as she reluctantly paid Lucy for the lemonade.

Solution

The Mystery of the
Missing Money

Nobody stole the money, because Mr. Turner had faked the robbery.

"None of your story makes sense," said Hawkeye to Mr. Turner. "First of all, when you were standing at the bar, you were facing the mirror. If anyone had come up behind you, you would have seen that person in the mirror. Second, you said you were pouring yourself a glass of soda water. But the soda-water bottle is still sealed. And if you had fallen down, wouldn't your glass be tipped over or maybe even broken?

"You tried to make it look like the plumber did it by putting the wrench by the bar, but I bet only your finger-prints are on it," Hawkeye concluded.

"You're right," Mr. Turner admitted sadly. "I faked the burglary to buy time. I guess instead I just bought trouble. But I promise to get the money to you soon."

Two months later, Mr. Turner delivered the money to Mr. Collins. He said the embarrassment he had felt when Hawkeye found out he was lying had made him deter-mined to save every cent until he paid back what he owed.

Solution

The Case of the
Bashed Boss

Bertha was the person who attacked Mr. Hardy. She hit him over the head with a block of ice.

"See the puddle of water?" said Hawkeye, explaining it all to Sarge.

"You get it?" asked Amy. "Mr. Hardy was hit with a block of ice. Only it was all melted by the time he was found."

Because it would have taken some time for the ice to melt, there was only one person who could have knocked out Mr. Hardy.

"Bertha," said Hawkeye. "She went downstairs an hour before Joe did. And look at Mr. Hardy's empty wallet. She hit him over the head with the block of ice, and then stole fifty dollars."

Bertha confessed, saying that she had done it only because Mr. Hardy had been cheating her on her paycheck. Sergeant Treadwell later told her that if only she had reported that to the police, then Mr. Hardy—not Bertha—would have gone to jail.

The Girls to the Rescue® Series

Edited by Bruce Lansky

Here are seven collections of stories featuring heroic, clever, and determined girls from around the world. Each book contains tales about girls such as Emily, who helps a runaway slave and her baby reach safety and freedom, and Kamala, a Punjabi girl who outsmarts a pack of thieves. This series for girls ages 7 to 13 has received critical acclaim and raves from mothers and daughters alike.

Can You Solve the Mystery?™ Series

Twelve-year-old amateur sleuths and best friends Hawkeye Collins and Amy Adams love to solve cases. They invite readers to follow clues and sketches to solve crimes in their hometown of Lakewood Hills. All of the books in the Can You Solve the Mystery? series contain 9-10 short mysteries. Readers are given written and visual clues to help them solve the crime. The answers and a brief wrap-up are given in the back of the book. This series is for curious children ages 6 to 13.

⚄ Meadowbrook Press

6110 Blue Circle Drive, Suite 237, Minnetonka, MN 55343

www.MeadowbrookPress.com